BY BARBARA WESTPHAL

Pacific Press Publishing Association
Mountain View, California
Oshawa, Ontario

Library of Congress Catalog Card No. 80-11480

ISBN 0-8163-0359-2

Dedicated

to María de los Angeles de Cortez,
the Seeing Eye girl

Acknowledgment

For most of these stories I am indebted to "Macha" herself, now Mrs. María de los Angeles de Cortez. Others who have cooperated are Dr. Donaldo Thomann, Elder Chester Westphal, and Mr. Ananías González.

Contents

No More Fish

Mamá González (Goan-SAH-less) finished dishing up the soup into the children's soup bowls. She had already served Papá (Pa-PAH), who sat at the head of the table waiting to begin the meal. When Mamá finished dipping up the soup, she placed the soup kettle on the back of the stove and sat down with the rest of the family.

Macha (MAH-chuh), the oldest child, pushed her soup bowl away. "I don't want any more fish!" She made a face as she spoke. "Every day fish. I hate fish. Most of all I hate fish heads!"

"But, my dear," her mother told her, "the fish is good for your papá. Most of all, the fish heads are good for him. So we must all eat fish every day. That's why we left home and came down here to live near the ocean—so we could have lots of fish."

"I'm sick and tired of fish too!" Macha's brother frowned and pushed his soup bowl toward the middle of the table.

9

"Me too!" added a little sister.

"But, children, your papá needs—" Mother began.

But Papá pushed away *his* plate and said, "I'm sick of fish too. In fact, I never want to see another fish as long as I live." Papá began to talk louder and louder. "I tell you I can't stand to see a fish head in my soup. Its dead eye looks right at me."

"Well, I don't like fish either," Mother told the family, "and I *hate* to clean fish every day. But if it's good for your father's eyes, I'll keep on eating fish. I'll eat it, and I'll cook it, and I'll even clean it!"

Papá pounded the table. "I don't think it's doing me a bit of good," he said. "Really, I can't see any better now than I could last year when we left home and moved here. Sometimes I think my eyes are even worse."

"What hurt your eyes, Papá?" Macha wanted to know.

"Ah, my child, when I was at work one day when you were very small, I fell from a high platform and hit my head on the hard ground. Everything turned black. My wounds healed, but I have not been able to see since that time. We have tried everything," he sighed.

Mother frowned. "At first we had such hopes! Then the neighbors said eating fish would be good

10

for your eyes. So we came here where we could get plenty of fish. Maybe they didn't know what they were talking about."

Papá sat up straight in his chair. "Let's go back home!" He almost shouted the words. "No more fish! No more fish heads!"

Macha clapped her hands and called out the loudest of all, "No more fish! Let's go home!"

At once they began to make plans.

"I'll sell our dried fish and buy some fruit. I'll take bananas and pineapples home with me. Maybe I'll sell some and make a little money," Papá said.

Mother smiled at her husband. "You're always selling something, dear."

"Can we go home on the train?" Reuben asked.

"Yes, of course, the same way we came," Papá nodded.

"Chalo (CHAH-low)." Mother called Papá by his nickname as she put her hand over his. "Please go to see a good doctor—an eye doctor—when we get home."

Papá agreed to go as soon as they got home.

Right away the family began to pack their things.

In a couple of days they were ready. Boxes of food, suitcases, rolls of blankets stood in the kitchen. Pots and pans and lunch tied up in dish towels waited on the floor. The four small children jumped up and down with joy.

"Each one carry something," ordered Papá as he picked up two heavy suitcases.

Macha grabbed a bag of oranges with a big pineapple sticking out on top. She frowned. Then she poked her fingers down inside. When she looked up again, she smiled.

"Macha, what are you looking for?" her mother asked.

The child grinned, "I was afraid you put in some fish!"

Back Home

Through the windows of the train the children saw the last of the ocean. They saw the last of the hateful fish market and of the black buzzards flying over it. But they would miss seeing the white sea gulls flying about in the sky. They would miss also the banana groves and the pineapple fields.

As the train chugged up into the mountains, Papá told them he used to be a fireman on a train like the one they were on.

"What's that?" Macha asked.

"The fireman has to shovel coal into the firebox that heats the water to make the steam engine go. It's a hot, hot job, and a dirty one too. Always shoveling coal. It was hard work, but I've always been plenty strong."

Macha and the other children looked at their father's broad chest and sturdy legs. "Yes," Macha thought, "our father is a strong man, not very tall, but strong and good-looking too."

As they came up into higher country, they saw hills covered with pine trees and very large oaks. Then they came out onto a high tableland. The children pressed their noses against the windows as the capital city of Costa Rica (COAS-ta REEK-ah) came into view.

In a few minutes the train had stopped, and the family hurried off with the bags and boxes, bedrolls and suitcases—but no fish! They all climbed onto a crowded bus and were at last almost home again.

When they got off the bus, Mother counted the children. "Here's Reuben, here's Macha, here's Rosario (Roa-SAHR-ee-o); and I have baby Gladys in my arms. All four of you are here!"

Loaded down with their bags and boxes and other things, the family began their walk from the bus stop to their old home, which was across the road from the cemetery. As they walked, neighbors and friends came out to greet them. Each neighbor expressed sorrow that Chalo González's eyesight had not improved.

"How this little lady has grown!" Señor García (Sen-YOR Gahr-SEE-ah) called out as he tossed Macha up in the air. "What's your name, little one?" he joked.

Macha knew he knew her name, but she was willing to tell him again.

She repeated her real name, Mary of the Angels.

14

Then came her father's last name and her mother's last name. At the end she added, "To serve you!" *(María de los Angeles González y Vargas para servirle a ūsted.)*

"You have a beautiful name," the neighbor told her. "Mary is the name of Jesus' mother."

"Yes, I know," she answered. "But everyone calls me Macha."

She liked her real name, María de los Angeles (Mah-REE-ah day loas-AHN-hay-lays), but she liked best to be called by her nickname. Because of her light hair and her blue eyes, people called her Macha, meaning Blondie.

As soon as the family had settled in their old home, Macha's father went to work as a bricklayer, building brick walls and houses. Then he bought and sold fruit, wagons, chickens, horses—even houses. He had to do many things so he could get enough money for food and clothes for the family.

At night Macha noticed that he came home very tired. But after supper and a few minutes' rest, he was ready for his work in the cemetery across the street. He liked that job.

In Costa Rica people like to have big tombstones with pictures carved on them. Papá loved to carve stone lilies, or even tall angels. Since only an artist could do that work, the job paid well. Certainly Papá was an artist who carved pictures in stone.

15

Macha loved to watch him use his chisel. Many times she went with her father to the cemetery to watch him work, but always she had to go home early to go to bed.

As the weeks and months went by, Papá's eyes did not get better. One day when Papá went to see the doctor, Macha waited on the porch for him to come home. As soon as she saw him coming home, she ran to meet him, caught his hand, and asked, "What did the doctor say, Papá?"

"He gave me some drops to put in my eyes and told me to come back in two weeks."

Every day Macha would ask, "Papá, are your eyes better?"

But always Papá answered, "No, not yet."

After another visit to the doctor Papá brought home bad news. Nothing could be done for him.

Papá finally went to see other doctors, but they too could do nothing for him. From day to day he needed his little girl more and more to help him.

"Macha, can you find a small nail for me in this box?" he would say. Or, "Macha, please help me find a pencil in this drawer." Or, "Macha, please pour me a glass of milk. If I try to do it, I'm sure to spill it." And Macha did all she could to help.

Papá decided to see one more doctor. By this time he walked, or stumbled along, with a cane. Macha waited for him to come home; then she hurried to ask him what the doctor had said.

Papá answered, "Dear child, don't ask me."

She saw that he had no appetite for supper. After going to bed she heard her mother crying. She crept to the bedroom door and heard her father's sad voice say, "Nothing can be done."

When Papá didn't go to work the next day, Macha saw her mother's worried face. Papá said he couldn't see well enough to place the bricks in an even line for a wall.

Then one evening, just as she was taking off her sandals to go to bed, Papá came in, banging the kitchen door behind him. He threw down his chisel.

"It's no use! I can't use this tool anymore. Just can't see what I'm doing! Not even with a bright light." He went to the bedroom and slammed the door shut.

"What's the matter with Papá?" Macha asked her brother.

"He can't see to do his favorite work at the cemetery anymore. He is too blind. The doctor said the nerve is dead."

"What does that mean?"

"No medicine will fix a dead nerve; so he can't see. He is blind."

Blind! Blind! Macha cried herself to sleep that night.

17

Danger

The next morning Papá *seemed* more cheerful.

"Come, Macha, let's go for a walk. You hold my hand and lead me so I won't stumble and fall."

"Where shall we go?" she asked.

"Let's go down by the railroad tracks. We can watch the train pass on its way to Puntarenas (Pun-tĕ-RAY-nĕs) down by the ocean."

"Is that where we used to live when we had to eat so much fish?" Macha wanted to know.

"Yes. One train goes to the Pacific Ocean. Another train goes to the Atlantic Ocean."

Macha thought a moment and then said, "So Costa Rica is between the two oceans."

"Yes," her father told her. "The name means Rich Coast. The Spanish explorers called it that because they hoped to find gold. They didn't get the gold they wanted. But we have a land that is rich in other ways. We really have two rich coasts instead of one."

18

Macha laughed. "Then we should call it Rich Coasts instead of Rich Coast."

They made their way hand in hand until they came to the railroad tracks. The clock on the tall church tower struck the hour nine times. In a few mintues, Macha knew, the big train would roar by.

Papá reached into his pocket and took out a coin. "Here is a *colón* (ko-LOAN)," he said. (Colón is Spanish for Columbus; so they call their dollar a *colón*, or Columbus, in Costa Rica.) "Go buy yourself some candy at the store on the corner."

The little girl took the money and ran up the hill to the store. What a treat! She put the *colón* on the counter and picked up the two chocolates she had decided on. Just then she heard the train whiz past. She unwrapped one of the chocolates and stuffed it in her mouth while she held the other tight in her hand. Then she ran back down the hill.

The neighbor, Señor García, stood beside Papá. Señor García looked very cross.

"María de los Angeles," he scolded, "what do you mean by running off and leaving your Papá all alone right here by the tracks! You know he can't see. The train could have run over him. I came along just in time to pull him away from the tracks."

"But—but—Papá *told* me to go to the store," the child explained.

The neighbor looked at Papá in a strange way.

Then he went on to his work. Macha led her blind father home.

The next day Papá and Macha went for another morning walk.

"It's good for me to get out in the fresh morning air," he told her. He gave her another *colón* for candy. Macha stood still. "But, Papá, Señor García said I must not leave you here by the tracks."

"I'll be all right, child. I'll just sit here and wait for you."

Macha left him sitting on a big rock near the tracks. Again she missed seeing the train rush past because she had gone to buy more candy. Again Señor García stood there talking to her father when she came running back. Macha wondered why he was there at the same place and at the same time as yesterday.

She felt frightened when she saw the neighbor and heard him speaking in a stern voice to her father. She stopped to listen.

"Gonzalo González! (Goan-SAH-lo Goan-SAH-less) You can't do that! You don't want your little girl to find your body all broken. Your family needs you," he continued.

"Why did the neighbor talk like that?" Macha wondered.

Papá stood there hanging his head. "I'm just a worry to my family."

20

"Chalo," the man said, calling Papá by his nickname, "you are coming to church with me tonight. It's prayer-meeting night. You'll find life is worth living. God will give you strength to live with your blindness. He will give you peace and hope."

That evening Señor García came for her father, and of course Macha went along. She had never been in any church except the big Catholic one on the plaza. This church wasn't large or beautiful. There were no images of saints along the walls. Nor did she see any priest, nor any altar boy, nor did she smell any incense.

A man dressed like any other man sang and talked and prayed. Macha liked songs. In the past she had heard only prayers that were said by heart. When this minister prayed, it seemed he talked face-to-face with God.

At the end of the service Papá asked the people to pray for him. Tears rolled down his cheeks.

Every day after that, Señor García came to study the Bible with Papá, and Macha listened to every word.

Macha wished her father could see the book, called a Bible, with such sweet words in it. He could only hold it in his hands lovingly.

By the next prayer-meeting night Papá was ready to tell what had happened the week before.

"When I knew I would always be blind," Macha

21

heard him say, "I didn't want to live anymore. I planned to throw myself across the railroad tracks just before the train came by."

Macha gave a little gasp and opened her eyes wide. "Two times I waited for the train," Papá continued. "Two times I sent my little girl to buy candy so she wouldn't see me killed. Two times my good neighbor García kept me from ending my life—from killing myself. Please pray that God will help me, for I feel I can't face the future. How can I take care of my family if I'm blind?" he cried.

"Jesus will come close to you, my brother," the minister said. "You will have light in your heart instead of in your eyes. And if you are faithful and follow Him, He will take you to heaven when He comes. There you will see again."

Macha held her blind father's hand very tight as she and Señor García led him home that night. What a terrible thing had almost happened! She must take good care of Papá every day.

The Idols

Changes came fast to the González family after María de los Angeles and her father began to attend the Adventist Church.

Every day Papá studied the Bible with neighbor García or with the pastor. Papá had never seen a Bible. Macha saw him hold it tenderly in his hands. He passed his fingers over its form, over the gold letters LA BIBLIA (Lah BIB-lee-ah) on the cover, over the red edges of the pages.

"Macha, you must learn to read at once," Papá decided. "You are now six years old, and my friend García says you must attend the Adventist church school. There you can learn more about the Bible every day."

He turned to his wife. "Lía, you will make her the little uniform she needs, won't you?"

"Of course, I'll make the white blouse and blue skirt for her," she answered at once. Then her voice changed. "But what are you going to pay the school with? It will not be free, you know. I would think a blind man would not throw away his money on an Adventist school. The child could go to a public school free. Or if you want to send her to a private school, I'm sure the Catholic school would take her free. Our priest could arrange that."

Macha saw her father stand up straight. "Macha must go to the Adventist school," he said firmly.

The little girl smiled and thought, "He intends to be the head of the family even if he is blind."

Mother soon finished the blouse and skirt for Macha. All dressed up in her new blouse and skirt and black shoes and stockings, she went off to school. And she loved it! How fast she learned! After school she hurried home, and her father begged her to try to read to him. In six months she could read almost anything.

Macha had always loved to visit her grandpa and grandma. Often after school Papá would ask her to lead him to their home. He always carried his Bible with him. He would ask his parents to read the texts that he named. They soon learned how to look up the right chapters and verses. Then they began to attend the Adventist Church with their son, Papá's brother, and Macha.

One day the priest from the nearby Catholic church came to call. He found them all studying the Bible together.

"I brought my Catholic Bible with me," the priest said, "because I know you are studying a Protestant one."

"Our Bible is just like yours, padre (PAH-dray)," Papá told him. "But in your catechism you have changed the Ten Commandments. Look at Exodus 20 in the Bible, then compare it with the commandments as written in your catechism. You have skipped the second commandment in your catechism because you don't like it. Then you have split the last one in two so that there are still ten."

"Let me see your Bible," Grandpa said as he reached out to take it from the priest.

He turned the pages to find Exodus 20. Suddenly he noticed something written on the inside cover. Grandpa began to laugh softly. Macha wondered what he had seen.

"What's this, padre?" Grandpa asked. "You have written across the page *esta prohibida* [It is forbidden]. Three times it's written here. Why should the Word of God be forbidden by the church?"

"Oh, that is because it is very difficult to understand the Bible," the priest answered. "It is best for only us priests to study it. Then we tell the people what it says so they won't be mixed up."

"Or so you can explain it the way you want to!" Grandpa put in.

Macha gasped when she heard her grandpa speak like that to the priest. But Father Valenciano (Vahl-an-see-AHN-oh), a kind man who had known the family a long time, did not become angry.

"Chalo, what does that second commandment say in your Bible?" Grandpa asked.

Macha turned easily to Exodus 20. Then Papá "read" the verse. That is, he repeated it by heart. At the same time he pointed to the place where he thought it was on the page. That way it *looked* as if he were reading.

The others listened to the second commandment.

"Thou shalt not make unto thee any graven image. . . : thou shalt not bow down thyself to them, nor serve them."

Macha spoke up. "I know that verse by heart, Grandpa; and I know what 'graven' means too. It means 'carved,' just like Papá used to carve the stone angels at the cemetery."

Then she repeated the verse herself: " 'Thou shalt not make unto thee any graven image. . . : thou shalt now bow down thyself to them, nor serve them.' "

"So that's the commandment you left out of your Bible," Grandpa exclaimed, looking at the priest.

"That verse is pretty plain," Grandma said with surprise; "and all my life I've been bowing down to images and praying to them too."

"Just look at this room," Grandma continued. "It's full of images. There's my dear little Virgin Mary that I have loved and said prayers to all my life. And there's our good Saint Anthony on the shelf." Grandma pointed to the wall. "And there on the wall is the pretty picture of the Anima Solo (AHN-ee-mah SO-lo). You see we always keep a candle burning in front of it. When my aunt died, we said prayers before it for nine days so her spirit could go to heaven."

"Yes," the priest added, "the Anima Solo is a very special saint—the Spirit itself. That's a pretty picture of it going to heaven just as we do when we die."

"Oh, Padre Valenciano, you know that is not true!" Papá took the Bible from Grandpa. He turned the pages toward the middle, where he thought the book of Ecclesiastes must be. Then he repeated by heart the fifth verse in chapter 9: " 'For the living know that they shall die: but the dead know not any thing.' So you see," Papá explained, "dead people don't know anything. There is nothing going up to heaven when a person dies. They rest in their graves until Jesus comes. *That* is what the Bible says."

"Papá," Macha spoke up. "Read him the verses that say that images can't hear or see."

"Yes, my girl, you are learning fast. Those verses are in Isaiah."

Papá turned the pages and then said, "In Isaiah 45:20 I read, 'They have no knowledge that set up the wood of their graven image, or pray unto a god that cannot save.' "

The priest stood up to leave saying, "I shall not argue with you, Gonzalo González."

As soon as he had gone, Grandpa and Grandma began to carry the images outdoors. Macha helped.

"Let's burn them!" Grandpa said.

"Or break them!" Grandma added as she carried out a little china idol.

The fire and the hammer soon did their work. When the images had been destroyed, the family came back into Grandpa's house for prayer.

Macha listened while Grandpa prayed. "Dear God, forgive us for worshiping idols. We know You are the only God, though we cannot see You. Give us faith. Hear our prayers. Amen."

When the old man had prayed, he got up from his knees, and there on the table lay the priest's Bible. "Ha! Ha!" He smiled a big smile. "Father Valenciano left his Bible here!"

"Give it to me," Papá said. "I'll ask him if I may keep it. You may carry it home, Macha."

The girl took it in one hand as she gave her other hand to her father and led him home.

Next day when Macha came back from school, her father smiled as he told her, "Father Valenciano let me keep the Bible. Now I can use a Catholic Bible when I study with my friends."

"And one that says IT IS FORBIDDEN three times." Macha laughed.

Papá Takes a Stand

Not long after the images were burned at Grandpa's house, Macha's father, Gonzalo González, was baptized in a river near San José, where he lived. Macha's grandparents were baptized the same day. Pastor Chester Westphal led blind Papá into the water. Then he said the solemn words, "I now baptize you in the name of the Father, the Son, and the Holy Ghost."

Macha watched from the shore, wishing she were old enough to be baptized too.

In the church she heard her father tell others, "I was blind, and now I see. If I hadn't become blind, I might not have found Jesus and this church. So I rejoice in my blindness."

Macha had learned to love Jesus too. But, alas, her mother wanted no part of the Adventist Church.

"Don't talk to me about it!" she shouted at her husband. "You are leaving our great mother church for a small, poor one. It doesn't let you eat pork or drink coffee. And you couldn't work on Saturday even if you were able to get a job. How we need the money now, with a new baby to feed! And here you waste the money on that little old church school. Macha could be in a big Catholic school, and we wouldn't have to pay all that money.

One day when Macha went to the door, she found a strange man there.

"May I speak to Gonzalo González?" he asked.

Macha called her father, then stayed close by to listen.

"I am from the welfare organization that has been giving you help every week because of your blindness."

"Yes, yes." Papá smiled. "We thank you for the help for our family. I have five children. It would be very hard to buy food for them without this help."

"But, Señor González," the man said, "I have heard that you now have a new religion. I heard you are no longer faithful to the Catholic Church."

"That is true."

Macha saw her father turn toward the open bedroom door. She knew Mother was in there with the new baby. Could Mother be listening? she wondered.

"González, the leaders of the welfare cannot keep on giving you this help unless you are a Catholic," the man said.

"But sir," Papá argued, "this is government help. It doesn't come from the church. And our government gives us religious freedom."

"That's true," answered the official, "but this is a Catholic country, and the leaders of the welfare will not keep on—"

Macha kept watching the open door. She saw her father doing the same. The little girl felt sure her mother would come rushing out and scold her father. She could imagine the words her mother would use: "How can you lose this welfare help because of that crazy church? Are you going to let your children starve?"

"Dear God," she prayed silently, "don't let my mother come out."

"So you must make up your mind, Señor González," the officer went on. "If you stay with the mother church, you will keep on getting the welfare help. If you are an Adventist, you will not."

"I cannot sell my faith," Papá stated. "I am an Adventist."

The officer left.

Macha heard the swish, swish of her mother's skirt. Now would come the angry, cruel words! Mother stood in the doorway, neat as always in a dress she had made. Macha could tell that Mother was angry all right.

"Did the officer leave the money?" she asked.

"Yes, but just for this week," Papá answered.

"Well, he might as well have taken the dirty money! How unfair! It should make no difference what your religion is. You are blind, and you deserve the help. You did right to tell him the truth!" She stamped her foot. "I tell you, we don't even want their old money. I'll sew. I'll take in washing. We'll make it on our own."

"Lía," Macha heard her father say softly, "you are a noble woman!"

Macha often helped her father with little chores or with buying and selling, or picking up washing for mother. Now she and her father decided on a new plan to earn money when she came home from school.

"We will sell *Centinelas!*" her father told her. "You will help me, Macha."

"Centi—? What's that?" Macha wanted to know.

"The *Centinela* is a Christian magazine. We will earn a little bit every time we sell one. But we will also be finding people who want to know more about the Bible."

Together Macha and Papá walked all over the city of San José. Up and down the streets they went with the magazines in their hands, politely offering the paper for half a *colón*.

Sometimes they took the bus and went to the town of Alajuela (Ă-lah-hway-la) and went from door to

33

door there. In that town they could sell 100 magazines in one day.

"We're not making much money," her father often told Macha. "But the papers have a message. Some of the people that read them will ask questions, and then we can study the Bible with them."

Soon they had regular customers. A favorite stop for Macha was at a large bakery on the main street of Alajuela. Every time she ran in with the *Centinela*, the lady gave her a long loaf of Italian bread. It was always hot and golden crusty on the outside, soft and white inside.

Later Macha and Papá began to sell Christian books too. Papá became a fine book salesman.

Macha continued to learn fast in school. She had to! Her father kept her reading all the time.

"Little daughter," he would say, "I have here some printed Bible studies. Please find the one about the Sabbath."

Macha looked through all the tracts until she found the one Papá had asked for.

"Here it is, Papá," she said.

"Good. Now read me all the texts so that I can memorize those references."

She read the list over and over until he knew it from memory.

"First is Genesis, chapter 1, verses 5, 8, 13, 19, and 31," he repeated.

She would remind him, "Then the fourth commandment in Exodus 20."

"Yes, yes, Macha, and then a verse from Mark."

"You skipped the one in Isaiah 58:13, 14."

"Ah, yes, then the one in Ezekiel. I'm sure I won't forget the ones in Luke and John. That makes eight good ones."

When he had memorized the texts, she looked them all up and read the verses to him. Over and over she read each verse as he repeated it after her. What a memory he had! Soon the verses were in his mind, word for word, never to be forgotten.

They were in Macha's mind too!

Not only did Macha read the Bible to him; but as she grew older, she read entire books—books like *The Great Controversy* and *The Desire of Ages.*

About two years after Papá's baptism, Pastor Westphal made another visit to the church in San José. After Sabbath School Macha led her papá into the ministers' room. There Pastor Westphal met him.

"Chalo, I'm so glad to see you again!" Pastor Westphal exclaimed as he gave the blind man a big hug in true Spanish style.

"And I am pleased to greet you again, Pastor Westphal," Papá said.

"How did you know me?" Pastor Westphal asked.

"By your voice, of course. It's been two years since I heard that voice at my baptism, but I shall never forget it. And now," he added, "my wife Lía has been baptized too. We have a happy Adventist home now, and she is a great help to me.

"My daughter Macha is always by my side. We are all in the church. I know the members and their problems. I visit them and study with them, and we also sell Adventist books and give Bible studies to new people too."

"You are wonderful, you and your daughter," the pastor said when he heard all this.

"God is wonderful to me," the blind man answered as he patted Macha's curly head, "and I thank him for my María de los Angeles. She is like an angel to me."

A Snake in the Bananas

"Today is Thursday, Papá," Macha reminded her father. "It's the day to go to the market and pick up our order of bananas."

"You never forget, do you?" Papá smiled at Macha.

"Well, I like to sell bananas, and I like to eat them. That makes it easy to remember."

Macha's father had several big stalks of bananas sent to him every week from Puntarenas where the family had lived near the ocean. Bananas grew well in that hot coastland.

At the big central market Macha and her Papá got their order of bananas. The big stalks were about as long as Macha was tall. They were very heavy to load into the oxcart. Every stalk had many bunches of bananas on its stem. All of them grew pointing upward. They called the bunches "hands" because the bananas branched out like fingers on a hand.

"What kind of bananas do you like best?" Macha asked as they jogged home in the oxcart.

Papá said he liked the big long plantains that Macha's mother fried or roasted.

"I like those too," Macha agreed, "especially when they are so ripe that they are black. But I don't like boiled plantains so much."

"Which kind of raw bananas do you like best?" her father asked.

"Well, I like the fat, rosy ones and the tiny yellow ones and the ones that taste like pineapples and the ones that taste like apples and the ones that—"

"Dear me! I guess they are *all* your favorites." Papá laughed.

Near their house Papá had built a fruit stand with a shed behind it. They hung the big stalks on hooks in the shed.

"Now we'll put the green ones in the barrels to ripen," Papá said. "I'll cut them off, and you pack them away.

He cut off the "hands" with a sharp, curved knife. He could do that himself, even without seeing, as he ran his fingers along the big stem, feeling where to cut under the "hands."

As he cut off the hard, green "hands," Macha put them in the barrels. Then she covered the barrels with gunny sacks. Just enough light and air got through to make the bananas ripen to yellow gold.

"Why don't they send us ripe bananas instead of these green ones," the girl asked.

"The ripe ones wouldn't keep well. Besides, they would get bruised on the way. Bananas are always picked green to be shipped."

Macha took out some bananas that were already ripe and put them on the counter to sell.

One day when she stood behind the counter arranging the bananas, her father shouted at her from the shed.

"Macha, come quick!"

She ran to him.

There he stood, knife in hand, arms up.

"What is in here, Macha? Look fast, I was cutting off a "hand," when I felt something cold and smooth. A rat would have jumped down and run away, but this thing—"

Macha gasped, "It's a snake, Papá! A big one!"

There it was on the floor, slipping out from behind a barrel. It was shooting out its tongue and beginning to coil.

"Slam the door shut so it won't get away, and call a neighbor," Papá told her as he backed out the door.

Macha rushed to the neighbor's house, shouting for help. Immediately a man came running with a big knife.

"That's a big one!" exclaimed the neighbor when the scare was over and the snake had been killed. "It's all of six feet long."

"I don't know what kind of snake it is. Let's send it to a laboratory and ask if it is a poisonous one."

Word soon came back that the snake was poisonous. "Very poisonous. It's a coral snake called 'velvet.' They don't live around here at all. Where on earth did you find it?"

"It must have come all the way up from Puntarenas wrapped around the stem of a stalk of bananas."

"You could have died from the bite of such a one. Somebody must have been taking care of you and your little girl," the man from the laboratory said.

"Jesus takes care of us," Macha told the man.

Macha's father and mother decided that at eleven she was old enough to be baptized. Pastor Orley Ford led her into the river and baptized her. She felt very happy after her baptism.

She continued each day helping her father. She was his seeing-eye girl. As they walked up and down the dimly lighted streets of San José at night, she felt no fear. She knew the angels would take care of them when they were giving Bible studies and helping others.

Once a week they used to go on a bus to Alajuela,

where her father had a Sunday-night meeting in the church. The last bus back to San José left at 10:00 p.m. They were always careful to be at the right street corner before that time.

However, for some reason one night they missed the bus.

"That was the last bus," Gonzalo González told Macha, as they heard it rumble in the distance. "What shall we do?"

"Let's walk."

"Do you know how far it is, daughter? It's several miles from here."

"Ah, yes, Papá, I know. There are dangers along the way. There are many thieves. But we need have no fear."

"Yes," Papá sighed. "But you are such a young girl. You could be stolen away by rough men, especially with only a blind man to protect you."

"But God has promised that His angels will protect us," Macha said. "Come, Papá."

After walking along for over an hour, Macha saw a light coming nearer. They heard a horse's hooves clatter on the stone road.

"That must be the *ronda*," Papá said.

"The what?" Macha asked.

"The policeman on horseback making his rounds."

The policeman stopped beside them and shone

41

his light on the girl's fair hair.

"What are you doing at this time of night with this young girl?" the policeman asked roughly.

"Sir, this young girl is my daughter. I have been holding a meeting in the church in Alajuela. We missed the last bus. We are walking to our home in San José. We live in the part called Cuba, near the cemetery."

"And my father is blind," added Macha.

The policeman's stern voice changed. "I will go with you and protect you," he told them.

After a while he asked, "Aren't you afraid to live by the cemetery?"

"Oh, no," Macha answered.

Then Papá explained that the dead are sleeping till Jesus comes. "There are no ghosts floating around!"

All the way to San José and across the city to their home, the mounted policeman stayed with them. He shone his light on the road as Macha led her father.

"That policeman really took care of us tonight, didn't he?" Macha said when they at last were inside the house.

"God put it in his heart, my daughter," her father replied. "We must thank Him."

No Children Allowed

One day Papá called Macha to go with him to visit the lepers who lived in a leper colony a few miles away.

"Lepers, Papá?" Macha exclaimed. "Oh, Papá, aren't you afraid to go there?"

"No, my child. God will protect us."

Macha's mother spoke up sharply to her husband. "Chalo," she said, "you certainly aren't planning to take that child with you."

"Who else?" Chalo answered. "This morning in Sabbath School one of our new members, Alicia Selva, asked me to go and see her brother in the leper colony. She is afraid he hasn't long to live. He could die without any hope of heaven. I must go to see him and tell him about the loving Jesus. I promised Alicia I would visit him. She is going to meet us there. We must be at the colony entrance by three o'clock."

"Well," Mother said, "if you feel you must go, at

least take along a bottle of alcohol with you and wash your hands well with it when you leave. Promise me you won't touch the lepers, Chalo," Mother added.

She got a bottle of alcohol and a clean handkerchief and gave it to Papá. "Now see to it you wash your hands well when you leave the colony, and, Chalo, be sure Macha washes her hands well with the alcohol too."

Father put the alcohol and the handkerchief in his pocket, and placing his hand on Macha's shoulder, he suggested that they hurry along or they would not be at the leper colony on time.

As they hurried down the road to the place where they would take a bus, Macha thought about the lepers. She had heard many things about leprosy. She knew it was a terrible disease. But she knew too that the leprosy of sin was a terrible thing. Alicia Selva's brother needed to have the chance to hear about the One who could cure him from the leprosy of sin.

Finally they reached the leper colony. There at the gate they found Alicia waiting for them.

"Oh, I am so glad to see you," she said, shaking Papá's hand. "I was afraid you might not come. I thought you might be afraid to come here."

Just then a guard came to the gate and opened it for them to go through. But when he saw Macha, he

44

held up his hand to stop them.

"No children allowed," he said.

"But I am blind," Papá explained. "She is my guide."

"Sorry," the guard said. "No children are allowed. Let the lady guide you."

Alicia Selva took Papá's arm.

"No," the blind man said, "don't take my arm. You can help me more by letting me put my hand on your shoulder. I will walk a step behind you. I can follow you very well." Then he turned to Macha and said, "Stay close by the gate, my child."

Macha hated to have to stay outside the gate. She had felt afraid when her father had first spoken about visiting the leper colony. But now she wanted to be with him.

For a while Macha stood looking between the bars of the gate as her father and Alicia walked down the road away from her. After a while she looked around and saw a loquat tree nearby. Small fruit hung from the branches.

"Mmm. I love loquats," she said and ran over to the tree. She picked a few and then, after removing the skin, she slipped the soft part of the fruit into her mouth. "Just right. Sweet and juicy," she said as she ate her fill.

At last she went back to the gate and looked through into the courtyard again. Some lepers were walking around the courtyard. Some sat on benches. They all looked so hopeless. They were not laughing. Some had bandages on their foreheads, over their eyes, or on their hands or feet. Some were lame, and hobbled about. Many were blind. How lonely and sad they all looked.

Finally Macha saw Alicia coming toward the gate with Papá following with his hand on her shoulder. Walking beside Papá was a leper. His nose was gone; so were his fingertips and his toes. Macha shuddered as she looked at this man. This must be Alicia Selva's brother, whom they had come to see.

As they came nearer the gate, she saw that this man with no nose, and who had no fingertips or toes, was smiling. Then at the gate Papá turned to the man and threw his arms around him. He gave the man a big hug and a pat on the back in true Spanish style. Then he took the man's hand, the hand with no fingertips, and shook it.

The guard opened the gate, and Papá and Alicia walked out. Papá pushed Macha around the corner from the gate and took out the bottle of alcohol he had brought from home, and the handkerchief. After pouring the alcohol on the handkerchief he wiped his hands carefully. Then he turned to Macha and told her to do the same.

"But, Papá, I didn't even go inside," she said.

"Use the alcohol anyway," Papá insisted. "Some

46

say you don't get leprosy by touching a leper, but I don't know. We won't take any risks, my child."

As Macha, her father, and Alicia started toward the bus stop, Alicia said, "Next time we come, we must try to get special permission to bring my brother's three daughters from the women's side."

Papá held up his hands in surprise. "You didn't tell me the man had three daughters in there. How terrible!"

"Yes," Alicia said, "It is very sad. If we have a little Bible study group each week, I would like to have the girls attend it."

Papá promised he would make the arrangements so the three daughters could attend the Bible study.

Macha thought about the lepers all the way home. She couldn't keep the tears from coming when she asked, "Papá, do the lepers suffer much pain?"

Papá explained that there is no feeling in the part of the body that has leprosy. Lepers have to be careful not to hurt or burn themselves, because they can't feel anything in the places where the leprosy takes over. "It's the separation from friends and loved ones that hurts the most," Papá said.

"Maybe someday doctors will find a way to treat lepers in their homes," Macha said. "Wouldn't it be wonderful if they didn't have to leave their loved ones and go to a colony?"

At last Papá and Macha reached their own home again. Mother stood at the door waiting for them. "Did you use the alcohol?" she asked.

"Yes, dear, we surely did," Papá said.

"I didn't even get into the colony," Macha said. "The guard would not let me in."

"Then what did you do?" Mother asked.

"Oh, I stayed outside the gate and ate loquats. There was a tree nearby with lots and lots of sweet, juicy loquats."

Mother laughed. Then she turned to her husband. "Did you remember not to shake hands with the lepers?" she asked.

Macha watched Papá as he ran his hands through his thick hair. "Oh, my dear, I completely forgot," he said. "I said Good-bye just as I would to any other man—with a hug and a handshake."

Mother wrung her hands. "Chalo! Chalo! May God protect us."

And God did protect them. Mother need not have worried at all.

Every Sabbath after that Macha went with her father to the leper colony. When they got there, Alicia was the one that led Papá into the courtyard and took him to the little group that waited for the weekly Bible study. Macha stayed outside the gate and ate loquats.

When the series of Bible studies had ended, five

people had accepted Jesus and became members of the Adventist Church.

The blind man, with one of the ordained ministers, had special prayer for Alicia's brother when he became very ill. But the poor man died. Soon after, two of his daughters died also; but they had all heard about the wonderful Jesus.

"Why didn't God let the man live when you had prayed for him?" Macha asked her father.

"God knows best," Papá said. "You know, we prayed, 'Thy will be done.' Maybe dying was better than going on living with that disease. I think the verse that says 'He giveth his beloved sleep' is talking about the sleep of death for many people. We do know that God knows what is best for each one; and since we prayed, 'Thy will be done,' we must believe that 'all things work together for good,' even though we don't understand."

4—S.E.G.

Part of the Team

One day the tall figure of Pastor Orley Ford stood in the doorway of the González home. As Macha and her father greeted him, Macha felt that he had something very special on his mind. Soon the reason for the visit came out.

"Our mission here in Costa Rica has great needs. There are many open doors for preaching the gospel, but never enough money or workers. In Liberia (Lee-BARE-iuh)—a long way from here—there is an interest. A man by the name of Huerta (hweretah) sells Adventist books there. But we have no minister to send. As we talked it over in our committee, someone suggested your name, Chalo."

"Me? A blind man to work as a minister?"

"You've been working as a minister without any pay for some time, it seems to me." Pastor Ford smiled at Macha as he spoke to her father. "I know you could do the work," he continued, "especially with the help of María de los Angeles. As to your being blind—someone in our committee asked if it would be proper for a person with a defect or a handicap to be a minister. You know the Levites who served in the temple had to have perfect bodies. But Pastor Westphal reminded us that Eli was a priest although he couldn't see well, and he was too fat."

Gonzalo González laughed at that.

"Yes, Papá," Macha spoke up. "Remember Paul had trouble with his eyes, and he was a minister."

"Speaking of Paul," Papá said, "he prayed for healing as I have done. I tell you I have prayed with fasting and with tears, and the ministers have anointed me with oil. But God told me, just as he did Paul, 'My grace is enough.' "

"God bless you, my brother! Do you think you and your family could go to Liberia?" Pastor Ford asked.

"What about it, Lía?" Papá turned to Mamá. "It would be a hard trip for you and all the children— Mirella (Mee-RAYL-ya) is such a tiny baby."

"It would be hard all right to leave our home here and all our friends and the good school for Macha. We've always lived in the city. But it would be a great honor to be a minister's wife." Then she turned to Pastor Ford and smiled as she spoke. "We would be glad to help anywhere we are needed."

"Good! You know there is no railroad to

51

Liberia," the pastor reminded them. "You would have to go most of the way by oxcart."

"We'll manage," Mother said cheerfully.

"And I'll help," Macha added.

"I know you will, María." Pastor Ford placed his hand on her shoulder. "This call for your father is for you too. You and your father are a team, and we count on you."

Macha could hardly believe her ears. She was part of the team. They counted on *her*!

"When do we go?" Papá asked eagerly.

"As soon as you can get ready. The mission will pay all your travel expenses, of course. You will get enough money to live on. It won't be much, but you and your family already know how to be saving."

What busy days followed! Macha helped her father as he sold his house and all they had except the few things they would take with them. Everything had to be packed in boxes small enough to load into the oxcarts. Papá made the boxes himself, and Mother packed them.

The first part of the journey the boxes had to go by train to Puntarenas, as did the family. The older children remembered having lived in the coastal city. They made faces as they thought of all the fish they had eaten.

"I still hate fish!" Macha remarked as they talked about it.

From Puntarenas they traveled a day by ship to Puerta Bedero. There the book salesman, Brother Huerta, met them with four brightly colored oxcarts with covered tops, all pulled by slow-moving oxen.

The men piled all the boxes into the carts. One cart they decided to use for baggage only. The González family along with food and bedding that would be needed on the rest of the trip, occupied the other three carts.

Macha looked at the four carts and at Brother Huerta, who had his two sons with him. She frowned a moment, then said, "I see three men to drive, but there are four oxcarts. Who is going to drive the fourth one?"

"Maybe you would like to do that." Brother Huerta laughed.

"Sure I would! And I could do it if I didn't have to take care of the baby." Macha smiled and then looked down at the little one she held in her arms.

"Well, you'll see how three men can drive four oxcarts. We just tie the last one to the third one, and the oxen follow along without any driver."

So they traveled—the father, mother, and eight children, divided among the three oxcarts. They all sat on the rough floorboards except the driver and someone who could take a turn beside him on the seat.

Little Mirella lay in Macha's arms. The poor

baby had come down with whooping cough. The jolts and bumps on the road made her cough and whoop until Macha thought the little one might choke to death. She tried to hold her steady, keeping her so she lay flat as if she were in bed.

Eight days they traveled north into the mountains, stopping at night to sleep in some home or some wayside inn. Some nights they had to spend right in the wagon. A rough trip, indeed, but brightened with hope and cheer as they sang along the way. Macha led the songs as her tired arms held the baby.

The weary family finally came to Liberia, where they moved into a rented house.

The first morning after their arrival Macha came back from the market discouraged. "There are no vegetables at all in the market. What are we going to eat, Mother?"

"I was afraid of that," Mother sighed. "Maybe your uncle would send us packages of fresh vegetables every week."

"They wouldn't be very fresh if they came as we did, eight days by oxcart," Macha said.

Papá spoke up. "A plane is going to be coming in every week. I think he could send us vegetables that way. Soon we should have a garden of our own."

Macha did find one vegetable in the market—

something she had never seen before. It was the inside of the trunk of a palm tree. Heart of palm, it was called. It was white if she bought it raw, green if cooked.

"The sad thing about it," Macha told her family, "is that the whole tree is cut down in order to get the heart of the palm."

Mother served it in salad, crisp and tender, when it was raw. When she cooked it, the family thought it tasted something like the hearts of artichokes.

The family settled down to the new way of life in Liberia, but they missed their home in the capital city, which they had left.

When the Grasshoppers Came

Most of all Macha missed going to school. Mother needed her at home to help care for the baby and help with the housework. And Papá needed her more too, since they were in a new place. Every day she helped him learn new verses that he wanted to use in the sermon he would give in the evening.

They had a hall they had found and rented. Each evening Papá held meetings in the rented hall. There was no electricity at the hall. Every evening Macha had to light the big Coleman lamp. Once it stopped sputtering, it gave a bright light. Then she led the singing without the help of either an organ or a piano. If her father used slides, she ran the battery-operated projector for him. She had to watch carefully that she placed the pictures in right so they wouldn't be upside down on the screen.

Before the meeting Macha and Papá selected the slides that would be used. She explained to him what each slide was about. He wanted to know every detail. Together they arranged them in the order he wanted. When the picture came on the screen, she would very quietly whisper to tell him the title of the picture.

"The Second Coming," she would whisper, or "Joseph Being Sold," or "Eden." Once, when she said, "The Prodigal Son," Papá surprised everyone. He knew every detail of that picture as if he had seen it.

"See that poor boy peeking around the corner of the house?" he said. "He is afraid to go home. He looks to see if anyone is watching him. Then he sees his father waiting for him. His father's arms are outstretched to him. Then he runs to his father."

Macha had heard her father tell before how once he had run away from home when he was a boy. So he knew just how the prodigal son felt when he crept back home ashamed. He also knew the joy the prodigal son felt when his father forgave him. Remembering that experience made Papá able to tell the story with much feeling.

Usually Papá used about thirty texts in every sermon. If he forgot a text, Macha, who always sat on the very front seat, could help him.

"I'll be right there, Papá. But you won't forget," she always said when he worried a little about forgetting such things.

"Well, I feel much better if I know you are ready

to give me a word if I miss it," Papá always told her. "Try to find the texts real fast when I give them."

Every night she sat on the front seat. When Papá gave a text, she turned quickly to it in the Bible. Then she followed word for word so if he needed help she could say the word quietly to him. Of course, she knew by heart many of the verses he used, because she herself had taught them to him.

When twenty people asked for baptism after the meetings, Macha felt that God had used her as well as her father. Later sixty more joined the growing church.

The first summer that Macha and her family lived in Liberia, a swarm of grasshoppers settled on the ground. Like an army they marched from field to field, leaving not one green thing behind them.

Several of the church members came to Macha's home to see Papá. "What can we do, Pastor González?" they asked. "The grasshoppers will eat all our gardens. We will have nothing to eat next winter."

Macha knew very well what her father would say. He would say the words in Malachi about rebuking the devourer.

Sure enough. Papá said, "My brethren, if you have paid your tithe faithfully, you can claim God's promise in Malachi 3:11." He turned the pages in his Bible until he came to a place far past the middle of the book, where he thought Malachi should be. Peeking over his shoulder, Macha smiled because he had turned to the book of Matthew instead of Malachi. "Pretty close," she thought. "He's wonderful."

Then he repeated the text just as if he were really reading it from the Bible. "I will rebuke the devourer for your sakes, and he shall not destroy the fruits of your ground." Then he stopped to explain those big words.

"The devourer means the grasshoppers that eat up or devour your gardens. God will rebuke, or stop them. The fruit of your ground—"

"That's the corn, of course," one of the men spoke up.

Turning to Macha, he said "Daughter, you come with me. We are going to pray with these friends right out in their fields."

As always she took his hand and led him, giving little helps like "We're turning left." "Take two steps up." "We cross a bridge here." "Jump a ditch here."

"This is my field," one of the men said as they came to a corner in the road. "And this," said another, "Is mine, and my brother's is next to it."

"Very well, my friends, this is where we shall kneel down and ask God to keep His promise."

The prayer went right to the point. "These

59

brothers have paid their tithe as You told them to. You have promised to 'rebuke the devourer' and save their crops. The grasshoppers are eating up everything in their path. They are almost here already. Please don't let them come into these fields. Our brothers need the corn to feed their families. We believe Your promise, and we thank You for saving their corn."

After they prayed, they watched the grasshoppers coming nearer and nearer. Then they prayed again and watched again.

"Look, God is keeping His promise," the men cried. They told their pastor what they saw. The insects came to the edge of the field, stopped, then turned aside. Some went one way and some another, but none went into the fields of the men who had paid their tithes and prayed.

What a praise service they had in the church after that! And how the neighbors talked about the fields of the Adventists, that were still green!

The White Dog

One day Papá told the family he had to make a trip to the Lopez home, where he was to hold some meetings.

"Macha, this is going to be a long, hard trip," Papá told her. "We may be gone three or four nights. I could take one of the boys with me if you would rather not go."

"Take one of the boys? Oh, no. I want to go. Besides, I've already been to the Lopez place; so I can find the road."

Macha rode her horse ahead as she always did. Her father followed on his horse, and a rope tied them together.

All day they jogged along the rutted roads that wound through the woods from one ranch house or village to another. One hundred thirty kinds of snakes and frogs could be found in this part of the country. When snakes slid away under the bushes, Macha's horse took fright, shied away, or reared.

But Macha kept a firm hold on the reins. Sometimes as they rode along they might see deer, or pumas, or even monkeys.

Toward evening Macha realized she had lost the way. After having been so sure of herself, she hated to tell her father.

"Papá, I'm awfully sorry; but I'll have to tell you the truth. I don't know where we are, and it's getting dark. I've been a bad guide. What can we do?"

"Have we passed any houses?" he asked.

"Not for a long, long time."

"What kind of a place are we in?" he wanted to know.

"A real low place in the road. There are great big rocks on one side with very thick bushes on the other."

"That's what I was afraid of. I've heard of this spot. People have been killed here by bandits."

"What can we do?"

"We'll pray. Let's get off our horses and kneel down on the ground."

There on the road they knelt, and Macha heard her father tell God, "You know I'm blind, and my daughter is just a young girl. We are lost, and the night is coming on. You know that the Lopez family want to know more about You and that we want to tell them. Please help us get to their place. Show us what to do. Thank You for hearing our prayers."

They stood up and stood there in the road—waiting to see how Jesus would answer their prayers.

"Oh Papá, here's a big white dog! There must be a house nearby. Someone must own this beautiful big dog," Macha said.

"That's right, my girl. Let's follow the dog."

Macha patted the dog and began to describe him to her father. They mounted their horses. The big dog trotted ahead, and Macha on her horse and Papá on his followed.

In just a few minutes they came into a cleared place, and the dog began to bark. Chickens and donkeys and dogs and children all came into sight in the dim shades of the twilight. A father and mother came out the door.

The blind man asked about the Lopez family.

"Oh, they live a long way from here. You must have taken the wrong turn several miles back. Please spend the night with us," they urged.

"You shouldn't try to go to the Lopez place at night. There is much danger on that road. Come in and have a bite to eat. You can sleep here, and tomorrow we'll show you what road to take. Just come on in and rest. The boys will take care of your horses."

After supper the group spent a happy evening together studying the Bible. The family kept asking questions. The blind preacher forgot all about being tired in his joy at telling them about the Bible, but Macha's head began to nod.

"Here, child, you are tired out," the lady of the house said; "let me show you a bed." She kindly led Macha away.

But Gonzalo González sat up with the family until four o'clock in the morning teaching them Bible truths.

Finally the man of the house stood up. "We mustn't keep you up any later—or any earlier!" he said with a smile.

"It has been a long day, but a blessed one," the blind preacher told them. "I'm glad we got lost and found you."

Before Papá and Macha left the next morning, they sat down to a big country breakfast, gallo pinto, which is rice and beans, boiled yucca, a root vegetable something like a potato, and a special treat, iguana eggs. The woman of the house told the visitors how they had found the eggs along the riverbank, where the big lizards had laid them.

After breakfast Macha and her father mounted their horses that were tied together by a long rope and said Good-bye to their new friends.

"Papá," Macha said when they were on their way, "I wonder where the big white dog is. I didn't see it last night after we got to the house, and it's nowhere around this morning. There were other dogs, but not that pretty white one."

"I've been thinking, Macha, that the white dog was something very special. We know that it came after we prayed, and it led us to the home of these people who longed to know about Jesus' coming."

"Papá, what do you think? Papá, can a dog be an angel?"

"I don't know, daughter; but I'm sure an angel brought that dog to us. Or perhaps God made the dog especially. If the dog didn't live at that house, how did it know where to take us?"

"An angel guided it," Macha decided. "I'm sorry I took the wrong road."

"Child, you didn't take the wrong road. Your angel led you another way on purpose so we could meet that family last night."

That day they found the Lopez place easily.

"We waited for you until late last night," Señor Lopez told them. "We were worried because we know the dangers of the road."

Papá told them about the white dog that had led them to a house where a family needed to know about God.

Macha's faith grew every time she remembered that night. Both families—the one they intended to visit and the one the white dog led them too—accepted Jesus and became happy Adventists.

65

Partners

One day as Macha and Papá were walking along the street, Macha noticed a small boy sitting on the front steps of his home. The boy was crying. Macha left her father and went to the little boy. Placing her hands on his shoulders, she asked, "What's the matter? Why are you crying?"

Between sobs the story came out. His father and mother had been quarreling. They often had fights. Sometimes his father beat his mother and hurt her.

"Papá," Macha said, going back to where he stood waiting for her, "we must prepare a sermon on the home. People must learn to be loving in the family. What texts shall we use?"

Macha and her father worked so closely together on the sermons that Macha really felt she had a part in the work. They did prepare a sermon on the home that was presented over and over again in the churches.

Macha and Papá were real partners.

One day a letter came for Señor González. The blind man opened the envelope and then handed the letter to Macha. "Please read it to me," he asked. "Where is it from?"

"It's from the town of Limón," Macha told him. "It's from your friend Lucas." She sat down beside Papá and began to read.
"My dear Pastor González:

"I hope this letter finds you and your dear family well. We miss you very much since you left here.

"Since I joined the Adventist Church, everything has gone wrong for me. I lost my job because of the Sabbath. You know my wife is still a Catholic. She is very angry with me. She says I am without work as a punishment for joining the Adventist Church.

"Pastor González, I am very sad. I know you can't read my letter, but maybe Macha will read it to you. Even if you can't write to me, you can pray for me.

"Your brother in Christ,
Lucas."

Macha folded the letter and put it back in the envelope. Then she said, as if the letter had been written partly to her, "Papá, we must answer this letter right away."

"Yes, Macha. Let's make some notes. Then I will tell you just what to write. What texts shall we use first?"

Macha thought about Romans 8:28. She repeated the text, "We know that all things work together for good to them that love God." Then she added, "Lucas must learn to trust God."

"And if he has lost his job," Papá said, "I would suggest that he begin to sell books and magazines."

"Just as *you* did, Papá," Macha said.

"Right, my girl. Then we must remind him that being kind and loving at home is the best way to win his wife. If she sees a change in his life, it will help her to believe."

Macha was silent a moment. Then she said, "But, Papá, there's still the big question of *Why*. Why did God let him lose his job when he was obeying God's commandments?"

"Macha, my girl, it's that *Why* that troubles so many Christians. *Why* does God let loved ones die? *Why* does God let good people suffer with long sickness?"

"Yes, and I've even wondered," confessed Macha, "why God let brother's dog get hit by a truck and die. God can do anything. He could have kept the truck from running over that little black dog. Brother loved that dog so much!"

"Maybe I can answer your question and help Lucas at the same time. Write this down while I think of it, Macha. Then you can put it in the letter along with other thoughts."

Macha got out a pencil and paper and wrote down her father's words:

"There are many things we can't understand until we get to heaven. We ask ourselves why God lets us suffer. It is important to remember that God doesn't want us to suffer. It is Satan who brings accidents and sickness and death and bad luck. Of course, sometimes we suffer because we have been careless or foolish."

Macha looked up with a smile, "That's what happened to Brother. He let his little dog get out into the street. You had told him many times to keep the dog tied up, but he was careless."

"Yes," the father said, "and you remember how many times your mother has punished your little sister for playing with matches. She punishes her because she wants her to learn a lesson. She punishes her because she loves her and doesn't want her to get burned or have an accident. So God has to punish sometimes to teach a lesson. The Bible says He loves those whom He punishes."

The blind man continued: "Many years ago in China, when there was hunger in the country, a mission gave rice to the Christians. Everyone wanted to be a Christian to get the rice. Some who knew nothing about God said they were Christians so they could receive the rice. They were called 'Rice Christians.' They weren't real Christians at all. God doesn't want 'Rice Christians.'

"If we knew that good people never have anything bad happen to them, then everyone would be good. They would obey God to have good luck and not because they love Him. But God wants us to obey Him because we love and trust Him."

As she finished writing, Macha took a deep breath and said, "That's good Papá. I think that will help him—and me too. You really know all about trouble, because you lost your sight."

"Yes," her father answered, "I do know about trouble. What a blessing being blind has been to me! Surely I would never have learned to love and study the Bible if I hadn't become blind."

A couple of months later when a letter came from the town of Limón, Macha ran to her father with the letter. "Papá, here's a letter from Limón. Maybe it's from Lucas. Perhaps it's an answer to the letter we wrote. Shall I open it?"

Her father told her to open it quickly and read it to him.

Macha began to read the letter.
"Dear Pastor:

"Many times I have read the letter you wrote to me. I am learning to trust God.

"I have been selling books for a month now. God is helping me to be a good literature evangelist. Now I am glad God let me lose my job. He had something better for me. I am doing missionary work now, and I earn as much as I did before. Truly 'all things work together for good'!

"Also I must tell you that my wife is attending the church now. She is beginning to study God's Word."

The blind man smiled. "Thank God!" he exclaimed.

Home Becomes a Prison

One day a policeman came to the González home. Macha went to the door. Then she went to tell her father who had come to the house.

"Is anything wrong?" Papá asked the policeman.

"Yes," the policeman answered. "Your son is in the park. He is bothering and teasing the boys who are shining shoes there."

"Oh," Papá said. "I will go right away and get him. I am so sorry he is causing trouble. Thank you for telling me. I will certainly punish him, and I am sure this will never happen again."

When the policeman left, Papá asked Macha to lead him to the park.

In the park were several little boys called bootblacks because they shined shoes for people who stopped by their little stands. Each had a stool and a box of shoeshine and several brushes. The boys earned a few coins every day by polishing shoes for men who passed through the park.

72

And there Macha saw her brother, Reuben, knocking over the boys' stools and scattering their cloths and brushes.

Reuben evidently saw Macha and his father coming. He also saw the policeman who had returned to the park. The policeman got to the boy first, and he took him firmly by the shoulder.

"Don't touch me," Reuben shouted. He kicked the policeman, who lost his grip on him, and Reuben ran away as fast as he could.

Macha had to tell her father what had happened.

Poor Papá shook his head. "To kick a policeman is bad! We will find him. Come, Macha, let's go back home."

When they got to the house, they began to search for Reuben. At last Macha found him under his bed. He knew his father would punish him. When Macha found him hiding under the bed, he crawled out but then ran outdoors and disappeared.

Next morning they found him sleeping just outside the house. He had slept on the ground all night. Papá woke him up. He had a strap in his hand, and when Reuben saw the strap, he picked up a brick to throw at his own father.

One of the other children grabbed the brick away from Reuben.

When Papá learned what had happened, he was very angry. He took hold of Reuben and told the children to call the police. Reuben struggled to get away, but Papá held him firmly.

When the police came, Papá said, "You will have to take this boy and put him in a reform school. He is a disobedient son, and I cannot manage him."

The policeman took Reuben and marched off with him.

By the next day Papá was saying to himself, "Why did I do it? Why did I do it?"

The days seemed longer with one less child at home. The house was too quiet.

The reform school was not far from the González home. When Macha was clearing the table and doing the dishes, she would wrap up little treats for her brother. With the sweets in her pocket she would slip off to the reform school. Reuben would come to the fence when she whistled. Then she slipped the little package for him through the wires.

Macha could see that her father was sorry he had sent the boy away.

After some weeks they found Reuben hiding outside the house. He had run away from reform school. He had thrown away the striped shirt he had to wear at the school. He was afraid someone would see him and take him back if the shirt was seen.

At first the boy crouched in a corner. When he saw that his father was not going to punish him, he made himself at home. He had all he wanted to eat.

He slept in his own bed at night. But he was always afraid.

"Don't tell anyone I'm here," he warned his brothers and sisters. He knew he was a runaway. He knew if the police found him, they would take him back to the reform school. If visitors came, he hid under the bed.

Macha's tender heart ached for him. "What can we do, Papá?" she said after a few days. "He's sorry. He isn't naughty like he used to be."

"I've been thinking about it," he answered. "Maybe if I go and talk to the police chief, he would give him permission to stay at home."

Macha was glad to lead her father on that errand.

"You were the one who sent your son to reform school," the chief of police said. "If you think he has reformed, you can ask to have him back."

Papá and Macha came back from that errand very happy. Papá put his arms around his oldest boy.

"Son, you are free again. We want you to be happy at home, and we want you to be a good boy so you can enjoy the heavenly home some day."

With a sob Reuben said, "Thank you, Papá. I know I was bad. I deserved to be sent away. But I've learned a lesson, and I'll be a good boy from now on."

An Accident

One morning Macha suggested, "Papá, I have a bright idea. Let's do something special to celebrate Holy Week in our church."

"Holy Week?" Papá repeated. "It's a Catholic fiesta, you know."

"Yes, but it's in memory of Jesus' last week on earth. Palm Sunday, at the beginning of Holy Week, helps us remember the day Jesus came into Jerusalem riding a donkey. The children put palm branches in His path. Then Good Friday is for the day Jesus died on the cross. Sunday of Glory makes us remember how He awakened."

"Child, I think you have an idea there! I could preach each night of Holy Week about what Jesus did on that day. I could begin with Palm Sunday—"

"And end with Sunday of Glory," Macha finished.

The Friday-evening meeting turned out to be very special. Many visitors came. Some of them

76

wore black in memory of Jesus' death on the cross.

Macha chose slides for her father showing pictures of Calvary. She turned out the lights so the people could see only the lighted screen with the picture of Jesus on the cross. Then she sang.

"On a hill far away stood an old rugged cross."

That night many people shed tears and gave their hearts to God.

Gonzalo González decided after that to have special meetings every year during Holy Week.

Macha and her father made many missionary visits out into the country. One afternoon when they were riding their horses through thick woods, Macha realized they were lost.

"Papá, I don't know where we took the wrong turn, but we just aren't getting anywhere. I'm afraid we are lost, and it is getting late."

"No, no, my girl. I'm sure we'll come out onto a wide road soon. But this trail is bad."

The girl rode ahead on her horse, and her father followed on his, with the rope tied between the two horses as usual.

"Here we turn right," she would tell him. A little later she would say, "Look out for branches overhead." Another time she would tell Papá, "We cross a steam here."

That afternoon, as they puzzled about the trail,

her horse stumbled and fell, pulling the other horse with him, about fifteen feet down a steep bank. They were all caught in the thick bushes. Macha and Papá were thrown off their horses, who fell on their backs. They were mixed up with bushes and reins so that they couldn't get up.

Macha managed to get to her feet. She got hold of her father and pulled him out of the bushes.

"Papá, are you hurt?"

"No, child, I'm all right. What about you?"

"Oh, I'm not hurt either, but what are we going to do now?"

She tried to pull on the horses' reins to help them up, but they were too big and heavy for her. They kicked wildly.

"No one is going to find us down here, Papá. I don't think anyone rides along this old trail."

"We must pray, my daughter. Let's kneel down right here."

They brushed the dirt and twigs from their clothes and knelt down right where there were.

"Dear God," her father prayed, "You called me to be a preacher in spite of my being blind, and You must show us how to get out of here. You know we need to visit a family that wants to know more about You, but we haven't found their house. Now we have fallen down, and we aren't able to get the horses back on the road."

In a few minutes a stranger appeared on the trail above. Hearing their cries for help, he easily slid down to where they were. With expert hands he freed the horses from the heap they were in. Then, holding Macha's hand in one of his and her father's hand in the other, he helped them climb back up the bank.

Gonzalo González told the man where they wanted to go.

"You took the wrong path back there." He pointed. "I'll go with you and see that you find the right one."

In a few minutes he showed them the path they were looking for. Over and over they thanked him, and then he was gone.

"Who was he?" Macha asked.

"Someone God sent."

"Maybe he was an angel, Papá."

"Maybe he was."

Some time later they reached the house they were looking for. There they found food, rest, and a great desire to study God's Word.

When they told the family about their accident and the man who helped them, there was silence.

"God took care of you," one said.

"No one walks over that trail you were on," added another.

"God sent an angel."

Macha repeated one of her favorite verses: "The angel of the Lord encampeth round about them that fear him, and delivereth them. Psalm 34:7." (She always gave the text when she said a verse.)

That was a good beginning for a Bible study about angels. Other studies followed before the blind preacher and his helper got some rest.

Next morning as they continued their trip, they spoke of how wonderful it was that neither of them nor the horses had been hurt. Then Macha remembered something she had read.

"Papá, I read that in the United States some blind men have dogs that lead them. They are called Seeing Eye dogs. They are specially trained to care for their masters. When the blind man wants to cross a busy street, the Seeing Eye dog will stop and not let the man go ahead until the cars have passed. Then the dog will lead him across."

"Just the way you lead me." He smiled. "Macha, you are my Seeing Eye girl!"

Not Alone

As the years passed, the mission sent the blind preacher to other places to care for the churches. One of these places was Puntarenas, where they had lived when Macha was small, and where they had eaten so much fish. Now she was almost a señorita, and she had nine brothers and sisters.

She loved the fine beach on the Pacific Ocean, especially at night. While splashing in the cool water after a hot day, she would tell her father about the strange lights on the water.

"Papá, it shines as if gems were floating on the waves."

"That is called phosphorescence. There are tiny bits in the water that give out light. I have seen it when I came here as a young man."

"Oh, but I wish you could see it again. When I lift my arm out of the water, the little drops run down like colored glass beads. It's magic!" she splashed and laughed with delight.

81

The evenings when she could play in the shining waters soon ended, for her father and Pastor Orley Ford began meetings in town.

"Let's take turns," Pastor Ford suggested to Papá. "You take one night and I'll take the next." So the tall American preached one night, and the blind preacher the next.

One evening Pastor Ford found Gonzalo González sitting alone in a dark room with his head in his hands. "What is the matter?" he asked.

"I'm just making the outline for my sermon," came the answer.

Orley Ford laughed loudly. "What a fine memory you have, Chalo! I have to look at my outline every few minutes when I am preaching, but you have yours written right on your mind, and you never have to stop and look at your notes."

"Yes, Pastor Ford," Chalo answered. "I never have to turn the light on in a dark room when I am studying because I have a light inside of me."

After Pastor Ford left, Macha and her father continued the meetings. Hour after hour they walked the streets, making visits by day and going to the meetings in the evenings.

They lived far out of town because there they found a cheap house to rent. It would have been better for a blind preacher to live closer to the church. Houses in town cost too much money for the González family. So every morning they walked into town from their rented house.

Puntarenas was a hot, hot city. From door to door the father and the girl went, with the sun burning down upon them. They gave papers to the people. They studied the Bible with them.

At noon Macha and Papá had to walk back home in the hottest part of the day. Macha's head felt as if she were in an oven. By the time they reached home, they were tired out. But after eating they started out again. There was no car to give them a ride. All afternoon they went again from door to door, always with the hot sun upon them.

Their hard work was not in vain. More and more people came to the meetings.

Juana was one of those who gave her heart to Jesus.

"I am so happy," she told the blind preacher. "Now I want to tell my husband about the Bible. Please pray that Marcos will come to the meetings with me."

Macha and her father remembered to pray for Marcos.

After the meeting the blind preacher always stood by the door to shake hands with everyone.

"Good evening, pastor," a man would say as he took the preacher's hand.

"Good evening, Juan," or "Good evening,

Pedro," Macha's father would answer.

"How can you tell who we are, when you can't see us?" they would ask.

"I know your voices," he would answer. "Everyone has a different voice. No two voices are just alike."

So the blind preacher knew each one by his voice!

After the people had all gone, the blind man would shut his eyes and think.

"Macha, I didn't hear Pedro's voice tonight. Was he not here?"

"I didn't see him, Papá," she would answer.

"Then we must visit him tomorrow, Macha."

So the blind man kept track of all who came. He kept listening to hear the new voice of Marcos, and he kept praying.

One happy evening when Juana shook his hand, she said "This is my husband, Marcos."

How happy the pastor was to shake his hand! And to hear his voice!

After that, Marcos was there every night. A big change came in his life. No longer did he spend his money at the saloon. Now there was money for more food and for better clothes.

"It's so wonderful!" Juana told Macha. "He used to go to the saloon every evening. I was always alone. Now we have a different life."

Juana was surely happy, but someone else was very unhappy.

The saloonkeeper was the unhappy one. Marcos had stopped at his bar every night to buy drinks. He had spent much money there. Now he never came. The saloonkeeper was angry because he wasn't earning as much money as before.

"That crazy blind preacher is to blame!" he scolded. "Why did he have to come to town? He is spoiling my business."

Everyone knew the saloonkeeper hated the blind preacher.

One day Macha and her father were walking along the beach. The sun was setting. The ocean waves turned pink and gold like the sky.

"Papá, there is the saloonkeeper. He is carrying a gun. I know he hates you. What shall we do?" Macha asked.

"Don't pay any attention to him, child. Just think a prayer."

Without closing her eyes Macha prayed that angels would take care of them. Then she saw the angry man turn and go away.

The girl and her father didn't know what changed his mind. Later friends told them.

The saloonkeeper had turned back swearing. "That crazy blind preacher! I hate him. I was going to kill him for sure. But the girl wasn't the only one with him. There were a couple of men with him."

"No," his friends said. "He was alone with the girl just as he always is."

"Oh, no, he wasn't! I saw the other men with him."

Hate, and perhaps drink, made the man act crazy. He ran off by himself. He used the gun to kill himself.

When Macha heard about it, she repeated her favorite verse: "The angel of the Lord encampeth round about them that fear him, and delivereth them. Psalm 34:7."

Without Macha

When Macha was away from home, her brother Osman sometimes helped their blind father.

Pastor González had finished some meetings in the coast town of Puntarenas. He needed to take the train toward Alajuela, where he lived.

"Osman, it's time to go to the railroad station. Come and let me put my hand on your shoulder."

The boy walked along with his father to the station. He bought the tickets, giving one to his father and keeping one in his pocket. While they waited for the train, Osman wanted to buy a bottle of pop.

"Sorry, Son, but I haven't enough money. We still will have to pay for our lunch and also for the bus to Alajuela. When we get home, Mother will make us some lemonade."

"But I want pop now! Not this evening! It's terribly hot. I can't stand it without a cold drink, Papá."

"Osman, there is a faucet somewhere here by the

station. Take a drink there. It's better for you than soda pop anyway."

"The water in the faucet is warm," the boy answered crossly; "and I need a cold drink."

Papá heard the boy's footsteps going away. He thought Osman had decided to drink from the faucet.

The minutes passed and the boy failed to return. The blind man whistled for his son. He knew Osman would hear and know his father's usual whistle.

But the boy didn't come.

"That boy was mad because I wouldn't give him money for a cold drink," he said to himself. "But surely he won't leave me alone to try to get on the train."

The blind preacher waited. Osman did not return.

Five minutes before train time the bell rang. Five times it sounded, "Tling, tling, tling, tling, tling." Five bells for five minutes till train time.

Where was Osman?

The blind father began to pray, "Dear God, help me get on that train!"

Then, picking up his bag, he walked toward the train. He felt that his guardian angel was helping him.

He held out his hand until it touched the side of

the train. Then he walked beside it, feeling it as he went along. His hand touched the bar at the entrance to a car. He grasped it firmly and pulled himself up onto the step and then the platform. Once inside, he found a seat.

But where was Osman?

"Oh, dear God," Papá prayed, "let the boy be on this train too. I'll need his help when I get off."

The blind man sat alone for hours. He ate his lunch alone. His heart felt heavy. Where was his son? Would his son run away and leave him just because he couldn't have a bottle of pop?

"Macha would never leave me," he thought. "She is truly my Seeing Eye girl. How I miss her!"

Then Papá heard someone speaking to him. "Why, Señor González, what are you doing here alone? Isn't your girl with you? I often see the two of you riding this train to Alajuela together."

Papá recognized the voice of the train conductor. "My daughter is away for a few days," the blind man explained. "I had one of my sons with me, but he ran away and left me."

"Perhaps he is on this same train but in another car," the conductor suggested.

"I certainly hope so," Papá replied. "I will need help getting off the train."

"Don't you worry, Señor González," the conductor said. "I'll help you off the train myself if the boy doesn't show up." As he started to walk away, he said, "That boy needs a good beating."

After hearing many stations called, the blind man finally heard the name of his station. He sat upright in the seat, waiting.

When the train stopped, the conductor came to help him get off the train. He even walked with him to the bus stop and helped him to get the right bus. He told the driver just where to let the blind man off.

What the conductor and Papá didn't know was that Osman had been on the train all the time. When the train pulled into the station, he had jumped off when no one was looking and had sneaked over and taken the same bus that the conductor had put his father on.

When the bus pulled into Alajeula, Osman appeared as if nothing had happened.

He helped his father off the bus.

They walked home in silence, but once inside the house Osman got the punishment he deserved.

The Upside-down Bible

At last the time came when Macha went away to the academy at Three Rivers. Although Papá would miss her very much, he wanted her to have a Christian education.

The girl didn't have to study for her Bible classes—not after she had helped her father memorize all those hundreds of texts. In fact, she didn't have to study much for any of her classes because of all the books and magazine articles she had read to Papá.

Pastor Thomann, the principal of the academy, invited her father to come every year and speak to the students in their chapel period.

"He really can't be blind," Macha heard some of the boys say. "All those texts he uses! He couldn't possibly know them all by heart. Maybe he just wears dark glasses so we'll think he is blind."

"Listen, boys," the principal told them, "you watch this morning when he speaks. I'll turn his

Bible upside down on the pulpit, and he'll go right on 'reading' and never know it."

Macha felt proud when her father was introduced as Elder González, for he had been ordained to the gospel ministry.

She smiled as she saw the principal, with a wink at the boys, turn the Bible on the pulpit upside down. Gonzalo González picked up the Bible and turned to text after text, pretending to read as he recited more than a hundred verses from memory! Of course if he was "reading" from Genesis, he really had the Bible open to Revelation!

"You see, boys," Pastor Thomann told them later, "he knew them all by heart. Let's see if you fellows can't do a little better with the minds—and the eyes—God gave you."

Before leaving the academy after one of his visits, Macha's father went to say Good-bye to her at the girls' dormitory.

"Papá," she said as she gave him a big hug, "don't you want me to come home again and help you?"

"Drop out of school? Oh, never! I am so thankful and happy that you can be here," he said.

"But who takes care of you now? The boys always have other work to do. Rosario and Gladys are in school all the time, and Mirella is much too small."

"Mirella is as big as you were when you first

began to be my helper. After all, there are nine besides you, with most of them at home yet. I get along fine. Your mother has more time for me than she used to."

"Yes, but maybe you still need *me*," Macha insisted.

"Well, I confess I do miss you. We had lots of good times together, didn't we? But now I want you to study hard so you can be a worker for Jesus on your own." Papá patted her arm.

"All right, Papá."

"And remember, Macha, that you have had a part in all I have done. I couldn't have become a minister without my Seeing Eye girl."

There are many stories about Gonzalo González in Costa Rica, where the people loved him. They felt sad when he passed away long before he was an old man.

Macha still misses her Papá, but she knows she will see him again. When he awakes with new eyes, it will be Jesus' face he sees first.